# Talk Talk Talk

Retold by Martin Waddell
Illustrated by Mike Phillips

## Collins

2

"I wish I had someone to talk to," said Bill.

The door opened.

A giant **bottom** came in and sat down.

Two **legs** came in and
joined on to the bottom, and then …

6

... a **tummy** came in and
sat down on the bottom.

A **chest** turned up to join the tummy, and then …

... in came **two arms**,
which fitted on to the chest.

9

Then a big **head** came in and sat down on top of the lot!

"Well, hello there!" said Bill.

After that, it was
TALK TALK TALK TALK,
all day long.

# A Flow Chart

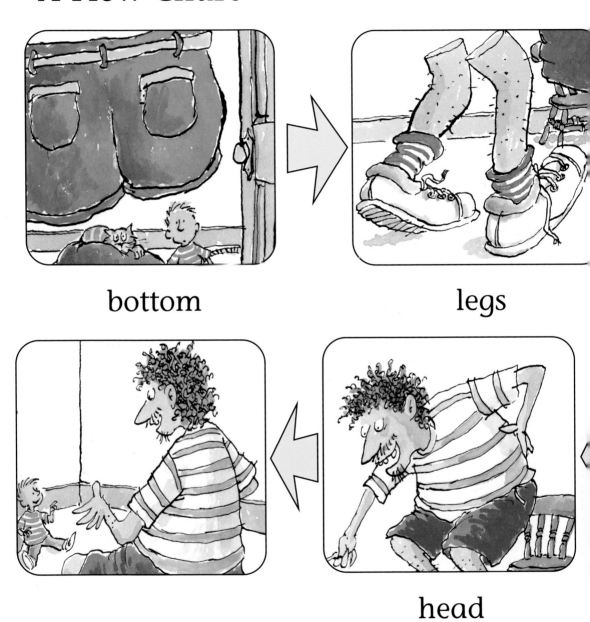

bottom

legs

head

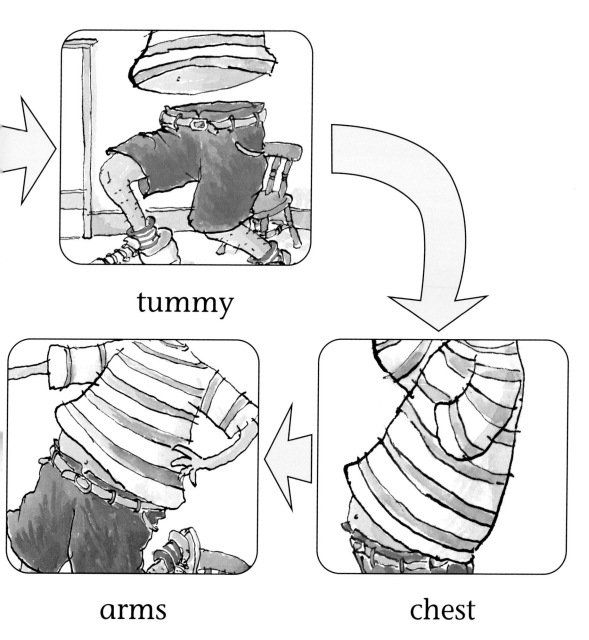

tummy

chest

arms

# ✺ Ideas for guided reading ✺

**Learning objectives:** to read on sight high frequency words and other familiar important words; to recognise ways to create emphasis in text, e.g. capitalisation, bold print; to retell stories, ordering events using story language.

**Curriculum links:** Science: Ourselves (parts of the body)

**High frequency words:** a, and, had, I, in, on, said, the, then, to, up, big, came, door, down, there, two

**Interest words:** talk, opened, giant, bottom, legs, joined, tummy, chest, turned, arms, fitted, head

**Word count:** 93

**Resources:** whiteboards and pens

## Getting started

- Ask the children to name as many parts of their body as they can. List their ideas on a whiteboard. Elicit the vocabulary from the story: *bottom, chest,* etc. Play a game using the list of body parts on the whiteboard. Say or point to a body part on the list. Children point to that part of their body as quickly as they can in response.

- Now look at the story together. Discuss what is happening on each page up to p13. Ask the children to find the words for the body parts in the story.

- Ask them about giants. Which other stories have giants in them?

- Introduce the bold print. Ask the children to find all the words in bold print. Are there any other typographical features that raise interest (capitalisation, ellipses).

## Reading and responding

- Model how to approach challenging words (*joined, giant,* etc.). Model the use of a range of cues to tackle these words (e.g. considering the initial sound, using the grammar of the sentence, looking at the pictures).

- Ask the children to read quietly and independently. Observe their ability to read the high frequency words listed above.